The Ding-Dong Bag

by Polly Peters   illustrated by Jess Stockham

Child's Play (International) Ltd
Ashworth Rd, Bridgemead, Swindon, SN5 7YD UK
Swindon   Auburn ME   Sydney
Text © 2006 Polly Peters   Illustrations © 2006 Child's Play (International) Ltd
Printed in Shenzhen, China   CLP100415CPL05150152
ISBN 978-1-84643-015-2
3 5 7 9 10 8 6 4 2
www.childs-play.com

Look at us! Two smiling boys,
Off to catch a great big noise.

Bong! Bang! Bash!

bash

Noisy noises all around,
Let's race out
And catch that sound.

Grab it, nab it,
Catch that din.
Here's a bag
To put it in.

Bash! Bong! Bang!
Crash! Crunch! Clang!

Here's a stick, and there's a gate,
Ding-dong-dang!
Don't stop - that's great!

Spanners in a toolbox clank around,
Unzip the zip, and bag that sound.
Clang! Dang! Clash!

Next, get wellies
For a waddle in a puddle,
Feet go stamp
In the stirred-up muddle.

Splosh! Splish! Splash!

Bucket, tin-can, garden rake,
Drum it, strum it, rattle and shake!
Gravel in a bottle
And dog's old bone,
Clatter and batter
That stick on stone.

Bike chains loudly clatter and clunk,
Football lands with an echoing thunk.

Bump! Thump! Kerrump!

We love loud and noisy noise
Better than the latest toys.
Thwack of ball on baseball bat,
Yowling hiss of angry cat.

Here comes thunder! Here comes rain,
Splashing and lashing down window pane.

Plosh! Plash! Plish!

If only we had room to store
The mighty thunder's throaty roar!
But, sad to say, our bag's so full
It takes the two of us to pull.

Heave! Ho! Humpf!

Up the steps
And through the door,
Drag that bag
Across the floor.

Hup! Ho! Lumpf!

lumpf

Are we ready? Count to ten,
Steady, get set, and we'll say when.
Now, mix it, stir it, shake it,
Squeeze it, please it, WAKE IT!
One more rattle
And one last whack,
Now it's ready,
so stand well back.
Whooaaaa....

With a WHOOSH and a ROAR and a WHIZZ,
And a finely shaken-up FIZZ.

Out pour loud sounds,
Little sounds, big sounds,
Whisper-in-your-ear sounds,
Very loud-and-clear sounds.

Snap! Vroom! Creak!
Thud! Zoom! Eeek!

Rip-roar! Ding-dang! Whizz-bang!
Bong-dong! Ting-tang! Fizz-clang!

What a dancing, thumping,
Ding-dong riot,
Till Mum rushes in,
Yelling, "Please be quiet!"

"No more! Stop now! That's quite enough!
Please put away that noisy stuff!"

Then silence falls as she shakes her head,
And whispers softly, "Time for bed!"

Crush... shush... hush.

So up the stairs we quietly creep,
And we get ready to go to sleep.

But after books and kiss goodnight,
And snuggle down, and close eyes tight.

Instead of silent calm, it seems
We're making noises in our dreams!

Snore! Scratch! Slurp!
Creak! Sigh! Burp!

Hooray for us, two smiling boys,
Fast asleep, STILL making noise!
Dreaming of tomorrow, when
We'll go and do it all again!